This book belongs to:

_____

Your name

_____

Your pet's name or future pet's name

For Roy and the humans who love him most,
David, Leo, Becca, Jeremy, Dylan, and Valerie —LT

For my parents, who believe
I always do everything just right —LBM

Only My Dog Knows I Pick My Nose

by Lauren Tarshis   Illustrated by Lisa Bronson Mezoff

Orchard Books

New York ∗ An Imprint of Scholastic Inc.

I always do everything just right.
Anyone can see that.

I eat every bite.

Even the broccoli.

I'm the best big brother.

I am always helpful.

And very brave.

I share my toys.

I never splash.

And at bedtime,
I close my eyes
and go right to sleep.

Except sometimes . . .

I don't exactly go right to sleep.

But only my dog knows that.

Only my dog knows
what really happens
to the broccoli.

Only my dog knows
that in the morning,
when I'm supposed
to brush my teeth . . .

Sometimes, I don't.

Only my dog knows
I don't share ALL my toys.

And I don't follow EVERY rule . . .

Only my dog knows
how high I can **climb,**

How fast I can zoom,

How BIG I can dream,

How tight I can HUG,

Only my dog knows I pick my nose.

Only my dog knows I never ever

SPLASH in the tub,

Except when T. rex wants to.

Only my dog knows
about my new pet.

And where I put my smelly socks.

Only my dog knows
why my sister really
woke up from her nap.

My dog knows me when I'm SUPER SILLY,

My dog knows me when
I'm extra WILD.

When everything goes wrong,

My dog helps me feel HAPPY again.

And at bedtime, before I close my eyes
and go to sleep, only my dog knows
that I check for monsters.

And check again.

And again.

And my dog helps me keep the monsters away.

My dog knows
everything about me,
and he loves me all the time.

And most of all
he knows,
I LOVE HIM, TOO.